ye shall know the truth

$$1 + 1 = 2^2$$

the math of God

saying through poems

it's time

for my equations

to be written.

61724

© toddymanners

Copyright © 2024
toddymanners
tbdg@toddymanners.com

LCCN: 2024914987

Ebook ISBN: 978-1-965064-66-5
Paperback ISBN: 978-1-965064-67-2
Hardback ISBN : 978-1-965064-68-9

All reasonable attempts have been made to verify the accuracy of the information provided in this publication

♡ credit to ♡

Alex Hinton Kuba...........
..... toddy manners the dragon
tattoo stencil
(inside front & back covers)

KINA .... armadillos
(with "this")

David P. Fox ....
.......an afternoon at Todd's
(between "the music" and
"...more shapes...")

———————

✷ ≡ for everyone ≡ ✷
who is, was, or hopefully,
one day, will be actively
working on finding themselves
within a program of recovery,
or,
anyone who does,
has, or
may someday
feel completely alone,
when surrounded by friends
or, always feels that way,
anyway,
I dedicate my book to YOU, and
I stand with YOU here today
where together, WE can start
and finish each day with
the "WEEEEE" version of the
serenity prayer. Keep coming back.

the important
stuff: → you're worth it.

this
is
what it feels like
to be whole.

Table of Contents

- - - - - - - - = poem continues

_____ = poem complete

- - - - - - - - = poem continues

_____ = poem complete

- - - - - - - - = poem continues
_____ = poem complete

- - - - - - - - = poem continues

―――――――― = poem complete

- - - - - - - - = poem continues

_____ = poem complete

my heart is starting

from the right place

of not knowing

how to speak.

another day of making
what's large
tiny
enough
to see,
and
what's
tiny
large
enough
for its
display
of invisible breathing
found in unhurried
beauty...

← this poem
(and the "24-hours" poem a few pages from now) is made for you to have fun with your color markers or crayons or whatever you've got for creating stuff. The same is true for any of the lettering you'd have fun coloring throughout my (now your) book.

← for Lisa ♡

amphibian

How are all of these froggies here
right now;
singing their froggie songs
like they'd never been gone
with all of that
scorching heat we've been having;
tarred roads cheese-melting
into becoming soft-shoe-gooey,
      at such brain-dizzying degrees
leaving no one
who could think long enough
to wonder
about anything,

while beautiful amphibians
wait patiently
within the earth,
for as long as it takes,
for it to start raining again.

Twenty four hours at a
time,

one year from
today

will look both different
and the same while
still growing every which-way. 42424

4-minute mile

our Heroes are just People who
went outside of the
had-tos
of what some people,
and what sometimes,
all people,
decided that other people
could not do,
resulting in showing
other and All People,
who also wanted to do that
one thing,
that
even if everyone says that you can't,
or that there is no such place
as your storybook-spot,
They Could Get Up After All,
no matter who says what, and
go outside of
"you can't do that"
too.

Battalions

put a photograph
of each of your
warriors and heroes

up on the walls of
where you live, and
≡one day≡

if it isn't there already,
your picture will be
right there

at home
with all of them too.

being honest

being honest about negative stuff
when it happens
means also being honest about
what happens that's great:
wearing my Butterfly shoes
Rainbow Queer cutoff-sleeve t-shirt
and long, bright Purple Hair
deep in the heart of wanna-be-just-red
Texas,
at a grocery store full of unpredictable
human people
during the midday hot afternoon and
seeing a woman approaching me,
as I wheeled my grocery cart through the store,
saying, "Excuse me...",
with me then asking
"yes, is there something you'd like to tell me?"
while she couldn't stop herself from
already smiling,
saying, to this six foot two 61-year old man
"You are so cute! I love your everything...
your shoes!
your shirt!
your purple hair!
I just love you!"
bringing her smile to me who now

couldn't help but to also start smiling, saying
"I love you, too!
Thank you for making my day!"
before we both walked
away through
the rest of our day;
changed people.

61324

blood kept warm

that breathing
you're doing
means that
you're not
   in a place to be told

by anyone
   (including yourself, 'cause
   even you can be a liar)

that it would be better,

for everyone
if you'd stop.

Bobby

—o —o —o —

It may look like
I don't run right,
But it's the way
That I run,
For some reason,
That only the God-of-Dogs has
The answer to.
So don't worry yourself too much.
Just get out of the way
While I run.
You may even smile
When you see me go at it
The one way
That only I do
How I do.

body language

my feet started talking again.
It happened once before,
while walking door-to-door
with a backpack full of missionary books.
in Hot St. Louis Missouri,
with no time for anything
other than sweating with the heat of
testimonies, books of scriptures,
And walking
And walking
And walking
like all of those kids did in that one
primary song about
Pioneers, walking and singing
while pushing their hand-carts.
We were doing that too.
My missionary companion and me;
our missionary shoes doing the talking.

Outdoor oven-heat insisting on
    becoming too familiar
     for the chaste,
we walked on melted blacktop;
surface conditions,
once hardened with conviction,
gone gooey with the sun
   as we preached about the promise
   of eternal life
     given freely from the Son of God.
A kid approached us with his friends;
   playing outside, together, saying to us
"Hey Man! You've got talking shoes!"
And we did.
Not noticing before; both of my soles
had come apart. Flapping happily
in the heat on their own, together
   and apart and together again,
        every step-stepping-step a
     teaching process of
two proselyters persevering through
the summer heat-index and miles
of Pioneer children songs.

My Missionary talking-shoes claimed
this sweet
unmatchable joy for me,
as I looked everywhere for people
who would want to claim, as theirs,
what they felt matched up with happiness
with God and his scripture-books.
I knew love was true
when I became a missionary.
A stick-full of dug-up gooey-road
    in a big glob,
    gluing both of my talking soles
    back together with road-tar
that would last them forever.
The kids smiled and laughed with approval.
I don't know what ever happened to
my Missionary Shoes,
but they never did fall apart, even
when I did,
two years later, getting kicked out of
love's understanding; too quickly
turned 40 years later,
being greeted by

the already beautiful Isle of Skye,
Scotland, with my best friend, Donnie,
showing me everything that I
always needed to see but had never
   known had always existed, including
a beautiful man,
      with a bright pink beard
outta nowhere
      from a thousand-year-forest
next to a cemetery, his pink whiskers
matching my bright purple mohawk

      perfectly

like a six-foot tall Scottish thistle
bristlebloom standing next to his
exotic pink-beautiful-flower-friend.
So natural next to each other,
      after having never met, now
riding away on his bicycle;
   stopping long enough
      next to a bus stop to give

a happy-to-meet-you-kiss;
    all of this everything.
The Multicolored Universe missionarying
    me, now, here
wearing non-walking shoes while
walking and
walking and
walking like a pioneer kid a
    purple bristlebloom through
    so much delicious beautiful;
writing song-poems with love from
my soul into my own scripture-book
    of found truths.
One foot registering miles more than
    the other, developing a blister so deep
it still says clicklepop beneath
    thick layers of skin as I walk,
insistent with made-up words
    a whole year later, inside of
    my foot, this time... grown from
wearing too-thin dragonfly-socksshoes

not meant for protecting feet from
Scottish miles of everyday and everywhere
of anything,
no matter how impossibly beautiful,
a deep blister, safe
within my deep-happy from
taking me to walking places
        so unexplainable;
what is exquisite does not come with words
that my vocabulary could know
how to capture... just
pull-the-car-over
and
stand within beauty for awhile
while spontaneously crying,.
    from never seeing
so much of what could make me unable
        to speak. I never knew that
a place could be...
            like this;
bringing unknown tears out of me
without even asking if that was ok,

before both Donnie and me are
back in the car, being pelted with
heaven's afternoon parties
   of Scottish raindrops
      large enough to drown out
         decades of un-salved brain
         scorpion-stings; those
gigantic Scottish clouds spilling
      all of their afternoon tea? Now,
just me and my
      bright yellow Nashville Warbler's

         happiness
tattooed on the back of my cupped hand

               window down
Singing its unwritten beautiful
songs, so many of them
      catching the flying-wind-current
driving through huge rain

thanking Drew for being there,
making it rain,
my tattoo bird friend flew
up and up and up to Kate Bush
singing Pi
for Kevin; then,
how to be invisible, for me,
thinking that
life is so beautiful I may never
be able to stop crying;
writing
what is becoming
my own holy god-book of witnessing
these missionary scriptures
and talking dragonfly shoes,
happy
that my best friend Donnie
has brought his own book for
writing about this time,
catching all of these new words

spilling
outta
nowhere
like heaven is absolutely frolicking
through another

Scottish afternoon tea

without having to be careful
about any of life's beautiful
truths spilling
to all the way gone

ever
ever ever
again

bookmobile

seeing a shirtless man
cartwheeling out
of a rainbow-painted
bookmobile bus
that has been filled to its
rainbow windows
with banned
LGBTQ+ books set for travelling
un-bowed all across
our very confused-about-freedom
country,
to be given to anyone
for free,
is the best kind of everything
that I can imagine
happening in our entire
multicolored Universe.

21

Bouncing.

Gay.
Not gay.
Gay.
Not gay.
Gay gay gay.
Not gay.
Gay, but not
Gay gay.
Ok.

crash landing

The tragedy
of a mama deer
wandering off for
food or water or
something other, something of
who knows what else
    she would be leaving
her baby or babies
    unattended for,
hopefully situated
at least near
some shaded grassy spots
with this heat the way that it gets
and then gone, sometimes
for a whole day,
or even two, leaving
her baby or babies
to wait for as long as

little bodies with
  cute little sun-dappled
camouflage spots that
  don't last forever
can wait, before going to look
with their tininess
for food or for water or for
who knows what else
they would be looking for
if not for their mama.
They don't,
Wait,
No.
They didn't know that
they were supposed to
ask any questions that they
  didn't know
  to ask
before she left them
Startled
With what to do

- - - - - - -

or with
what's supposed to happen next,
before their mama deer
returns
on another day to be
their mama again.
Everyone keeps saying to just
leave them alone
or their mother will never
come back for them.
Then,
too many baby deer days later,
there's mama,
pausing to look slowly, in both directions
for her baby
or babies, puzzling over
whether to begin with where
she left them ...
... right here
or
where

they might be
now. while
up that big hill
    and around two curves
her babies
have already been broken
and ground into
the road's
surface
heat like ashes to ashes,
by those big round rolling things
on those colorful shinies
going by.

Brave Shit

Remember that time
less than one year ago, at a
nearby city council meeting,
some gonna-shut-this-gay-shit-down
piece of shit guy
built up his gruffiest-upset-voice and
spoke of his confusion
about why THIS town
should allow LGBTQ+ Pride
to be seen as something to be proud of
rather than (the false equivalency of)
Honoring Fire Fighters and Police Officers,
the TRUE HEROES;
and the city council said
"You're right.
No to gay pride." And
        =within 2 weeks=
just-another-bullied-kid
at the local high school
in the very same town
killed himself, dead.

I guess there weren't
Firefighter or Police officer
false equivalency heroes sufficient
to keep another teenager from
feeling hated and worth nothing.

Mister city council
      shut-any-gay-shit-down guy
must be extremely proud of himself
for sticking to his guns.

Here's the thing about having Pride,
Celebrating our communities' true Heroes
who Dare to show support for apparently
Pernicious as fuck Rainbow Flags
in a fucked-up, backwards bullshit
town like that.
Sometimes, the chief characteristic of
Heroes, is the Bravery that it takes
to Be Seen as Who We Are,
Unapologetically,
in the face of hatred's putrified bullshit,
for Exactly the People who Feel that
   The Only Way to Survive
         is to keep themselves

28   — — — — — — —

invisible.
in their own local town.

Another teenager dead.
Another city-council shithead
                    Saying

"they're
        shoving it down our throats!"
        (always that image... as if, ever)

while they actively try
        to shove us out of belonging
          in our own town.

Rethink what it means to be a Hero.
Rethink what it means to be brave.
Then, with or without rainbows, maybe
the word PRIDE
        will have enough context
        to be understood by anyone
not choosing to remain
              willfully ignorant.

。*holy*。*shit*。

Every single feeling of being
at that dropping-off-of-life-point
finding me right
at the right pick-me-up-spot
right on time,
without me ever knowing how or
   where to find a phone book
   which apparently existed
      in ancient times
with exactly the right numbers
   for opening up to any page and
   pointing at anything
   with eyes closed, saying

Hey!
That's exactly what I needed to
   hear,
   see,
   taste and smell (at the same time)
   and, what was the other one...?

Feel!
Being in the Holy Shit
  moment of realizing
(even without those old phonebooks)
that there IS still something
that I can trust
that is still
right here with me
with all of its potency
in the present, being
  patiently silent
when   forget.
      I

Disclaimer

There is nothing within the open-blood-letting-poem-letter that I have printed here, in my 1 + 1 = 22 book of poetry, after this disclaimer, that I regret or wish to take back. This is my truth. Let it be known that, neither I, nor anyone I LOVE, or who LOVED or LOVES me, must have tried hard enough to fast-and-pray-the-gay-away, so that I could be a good church kid and make it back to heaven with my family someday. I am still a BIG GAY GUY; older, still alive, and with a whole bunch more perspective at a healthier distance (thank you, to my Higher Ever Lovin' Power, the LOVE that I have found in 12-step recovery, my beautiful Family of LGBTQ+ Humans who I-would-have-never-known and who I LOVE with as much LOVE as I am capable of LOVING anyone, and feeling ALL of my LGBTQ+ Family's LOVE at that same level to me, in return). What I was trained to believe, from the church leadership that I was born with and believed in, regarding LGBTQ+ Humans, and the LOVE from and for our LGBTQ+ communities, was, and still is, complete bullshit; nothing less than soul-corroding Spiritual Abuse. There are people who I LOVE and who LOVE me, who are still deeply involved in the church of my childhood, and who believe in it just as completely as they ever did. My open-blood-letting-poem is not written with any disrespect to any of them, or with harmful intentions to them, or what they feel within their belief systems. The poem that I wrote and printed, after this disclaimer, is intended and directed one-hundred-percent at the leadership of that church. I have been to more church services and temple weddings (waiting in the lobby) as an excommunicated church member than I can count. My LOVE for my Family and Friends has never been a question for me. The open letter that I have written doesn't change any of that. This is me, being honest with my experience, calling the deeply spiritually abusive leadership of my childhood church out, after 40 years spent finding healthier distance. I bare my testimony of this with my heart, with all that is true; LOVE.

Dear Mormon Prophets and Apostles
(an open blood-letting-love-poem letter)

You fucked up.
Just admit it
like you're supposed to
when you fuck up.
It's not too difficult,
and
that's what Jesus said you need to do
for true forgiveness.
Keep on reading, if you want to know
the truth that will set you free.
Otherwise, keep on
keepin' on with your
only-one-true-church propheting skills,
showering in tithing money.
That formula appears to be working
for you.

Let's begin with any of the brave among you
who remain
willing to see what happens when the Truth
Dares to disagree
with a multibillion dollar save-your-soul-corporation;
God "not being a respecter of persons"

sounds confusing. I know. So I'll help
heathen-'splain;

it means
respecting everybody, including so many
LGBTQ+ Humans, and their Families,
that You Fucked with your special,
inspired-men-of-god's-holiness-way,
smiting people's character with
well practiced
sleight-of-hand Fuckery.
Saying these
three little words
is a big deal, so
you can practice quietly, in private at first, if you like
(I'll plug my ears for a minute,
while you give it a try.)
"We fucked up."
There! You did it!
I'll admit it, I sorta listened while you were
practicing, 'cause I was dying
to hear what it would sound like
coming out of Your mouths
after all of this time.
It's ok to let the words sit for a little bit
and figure out how to put all of those
Big Syllables Together;
take you time
to really think about
how to say that you're sorry and mean it.
Every missionary flip-chart that we used to have,
in the good old days,
would turn to a picture-page and say:

The next step to Forgiveness…

(you know, like Jesus said to do
when you fuck something up
like you did,
but we talked about that part already
so hopefully that is in a place
in your consecrated brains
that you'll remember)
is Confession.
Finding the right way to
say you're sorry
is required for forgiveness to work right
because that's what it's all about;
the owning-it part of the fuck-up.
The Holy Hokey-Pokey when
you put your whole-self in
because, admit it,
Everybody in the whole world
needs and deserves
Forgiveness.
That's the whole Blood-of-Jesus part,
although (pesky-fine-print-found-in-truth)
even though the Gift of
His Blood bringing Forgiveness is Free,
        (even if you're already way over your
        eternal-salvation-budget,)
it doesn't mean that you can just put
        your confession
On a Platitude-No-Interest-Due
Corporate-church credit card, so…

Be brave and Have faith and all of that
general-conferency-stuff and

Just say it
Out loud.
You fucked up. You did.
The basics of confession, with
no need to thrash all about about it.
We all do it somehow.
It's just your turn to
Admit it,
if you're at all serious
about the getting-to-heaven-bit
without obsessing, for even a minute,
about who might be holding hands
at Jesus' feet.

The Worst thing that could happen when confessing
Out Loud,
the way that the Brave-Faithful do,
is still so much better than potentially
facing significantly lower kingdoms
(how embarrassing that would be!)
if you continue to refuse to
Own-your-shit. Meaning,
Own All-Of-Your-Shit,
not those mealy-mouthed-walk-backs like
"Black people didn't get the full privileges
and benefits of
Holding the Priesthood or having Temple Marriage
until 150 years into being the one-true-church because of
Yada-yada-bullshit-yada."
You get it. By the way,
way to not-bravely-admit the truth-of-all-things
Black, within your church;

leaving your bicycled-missionary-force to ride
All Around Everywhere, trying to explain
Face-to-Face, with sincerely wtf-wondering
Loving-Black-Humans searching for truth, how
All of that Nonsense made some kind of sense
in God's big White and Delightsome plan
(cross-referencing stretched-to-fuck-passages
of your own revised scriptures.)
Just fucking admit it
like you know that you should,
before the version of your Black-Whitewash is
still happening with "the gays"
150 years from now;
that same "yada-yada-
        we-love-you-for-who-you-are-just-don't-hold-hands-
bullshit"
from those who claim to be closest
to the source of God's Pure Love,
still not knowing a goddamn thing about it.

We may have to convene a church court
(of love) once you finally confess.
It's mostly a formality
to be sure, you know, to give an opportunity
for the higher-ups
who Jesus really listens to
to decide what to do with you.
Openly Baring Your Soul
is all that you'll need to do,
so, you should be comfortable with that part
of this painful
forgiveness shit,

with your well-practiced tradition of
baring
truth's testimonies.
Don't worry,
you probably won't have to go to any
Ex-Asshole-Full-of-Shit-Conversion-Camps,
  or have to
attach electrodes to your Holy-Junk,
while watching videos of what We find
        ZAP!
to be morally wrong with you.
None of that barbaric stuff.

You can trust those who are left of us,
  to not do to you
what you said should be done to us.

Oh yeah, one more thing while we're all here
in togetherness
at your church-court-of-love hearing,
before our loving-deliberation,
and our final, god-given-decision.
(Ya gotta Love the gift of Modern Revelation,
Am I right? It makes everything so much easier,
so much cleaner; just wait in the church foyer
for an hour of closed discussion,
after spilling your guilty-jism about everything
like I had to
    for two full hours,
        while fifteen of your
            white-priesthood-men-in-ties
                had questions for me to answer,

                    with their long, shiny
                conference table…
all of those blow jobs and butt sex
        with how many men did you say?
            and, were any of them all at once?
                    and you're still only, what, 21?
                                        Delicious!

        =ahem=
        =table-top-hands-please=

you know, just plain old confession,
as part of your forgiveness, and
loving Jesus and stuff.)

Here's a meditation prompt for you,
while you're waiting for god's close friends
to figure out
all-of-that-what-to-do
about you. There's plenty of time, with
the lengthy discussions having to take place,
for you to sit
on a church foyer couch and think
about One Question, that I forgot to ask
while you were sitting together in your church
court-of-love:

Did you ever kiss your Mothers
with the same mouths that you used to
condemn so many others,
leaving their own Mothers to
        Blame Themselves for

Loving
the wrong way;
unable to ever figure out,
with So Much Prayer and Fasting,
if the way that
they showed their LOVE
was too little or too much, or just
what-the-exact-amount-was
that your words-of-damnation
about Their Children
made them think that
Somehow
their LOVE was Too Fucked-Up
to save their own kids…
from being all fucked-up…
about such important stuff…

Your pulpits,
delivering Official Proclamations that
Families are Forever (if done the right way) while
You   Hack   Away   at   the   Family
Tree of Life.

This is the part when I say:
Fuck you
for what you did with the love of
my believing Mother.

And you say:
"I'm really fucking sorry."
Salvation made easy through the Blood of Jesus.

Thank you
for finding a way of being ok with
Not Always Being Right.
Sharing the Light of Hope to Everyone
that Forgiveness is Necessary and True,

even for you,

with your bare-human-feet on the same
    stickery-ground as the dirtied-up
"even-the-least-of-these" rest of us;
like Jesus.

Give yourselves another chance
at having a better vision;
rather than
making us smell all of your bullshit and then
US being the ones that need to ask for
God's forgiveness for how bad it stunk.
Modern Revelation, the New Generation
of Pharisees and Sadducees, with the
same smell of shit in the room for modern times;
        the nothing-ever-changes of
            a whole lotta holy butt-talk.

We will get to the very-rewarding
feeling-brand-new and all-is-forgiven
part of what's beautiful about forgiveness,
all together,
although, before that part can happen all-the-way,
I Want You to Know
        All of the Who and the What that

You Don't Know
about the
Suffering,
by So Many
due to Your words
that have nothing to do with

the truth of God's holy word.
Jesus bled
from every pore
in order to pay for the forgiveness it will take
for you to change
into a better version of you
that doesn't
Fuck people's Families and Spiritual Journeys in the Face.

You can do it!

There's no such thing as a know-it-all-box
so quit pretending.

It goes like this:
"We fucked up."
"We're sorry."
"We promise to not do it again"
then,
proving that you meant what you said
by not just doing
a wash-rinse-repeat to
get the smell out of your hair.

If you do it the right way,
the already dead
in LGBTQ+ Beautiful Heaven
may help you to wash their blood
off of your hands and say
"Forget it."
once you've really gone through those
three basic steps.
I think that you know them by now.

Thank you for your time and eternity.

I love you in a way that
loves the sinner and not the sin,
just for now, because we both know that
saying that kind of love is "love" is kind of bullshit,
like saying "we're better with it now,
as long as nobody starts holding hands."
    did you catch
          the love-drift
              in that?

Sincerely, one of your jilted exes,
    still attempting to convince myself that
when you said "love you more,
the way that Jesus loves
both of us"
you truly must have meant it… maybe.
I still believe,
hopefully in a non-stockholmy-syndromy-way,
    that we could both
get the rest of the way there.

Love, toddymanners

ps, it has obviously been way too long
since we've talked with each other.
Let's fix that part too.

Thanks for making a missionary outta
me. For real, there has never been a time
in my life that I haven't felt completely
grateful for that experience with all of
my heart. If any of you have made it
all the way through this letter-poem
of mine, to you, you will hopefully see
that what you have done, and continue
to do, to our LGBTQ+ communities is 100%

→ → spiritual abuse ← ←

Don't say that it's 'cause Jesus,
'cause Jesus and I are good. ♡

dead batteries
another telling-off
  of something so old
 is nothing new,
proving that in order to
get outside of the lies of
 "pre-established facts"
requires smashing solid concrete
testimonial
that, in truth, is already
razor-rock-jagged;
born-broken, then coated-over
for more silky-smoothness,
   with the dried blood of
     g e n e r a t i o n s
of feet
kept bare,
being told
as they continued to trod
  that jaggedy-path, that

This
Is the Best Place
That WE'VE Got.
I say to that,
Fuck that bullshit, motherfuckers.
Get out of the way
of us coming up
or Say no and get shot -
down, to the kept-quiet fathoms,
below
your safety nets and guardrails,
where
all of those
pre-fucked-up
"traditional-anythings"
kept all of the rest of us,
thought of as monsters
climbing out from
beneath
your featherbeds
with

the devil-teeth and blood-thirst of
all of your boogymen, as you scream
    about rainbow merch being sold
    at department stores again.
we'll just stay right here,
    eating non-dairy ice-cream
        while replacing your dogma's
dead vibrator batteries
and saying "grrr!" purse-lipped,
before leaving you shitting the bed,
comfortably heavy again, beneath
fascism's weighted blankets;
All of your Deepest Worries
spoon-feeding
unworthiness monsters.

—.—driftwood—.—.—

another

wave

crash

then

riptide

float

away

listening to beautiful

giving it a rest
for a minute,
just for this one time,
just looking away
from what wants to keepmebusy
again,
allowing
my mind
splashy-gulps from
adequately-clean
aquifers,
already
somewhat busy
at their own pace of things...
carrying a mindful
water supply,
all day
again
today.

...a few of my own moments,
to be left alone;

semi-refreshed brainwaves
quietly unzipping their tent

listening to beautiful

morning birds singing

their musical words...
            ... drawing me

into beginning
again ...

                    _for Dan

Dude!

THE BEST NUTRIENTS for the most
FAVORITE PARTS OF YOUR SOUL,
TRAVELING THROUGH THE MOST
ESSENTIAL-TO-EVERYTHING-
THAT-MATTERS PATHS OF LIFE,
GLITTERING GI TRACT AND S-
FINDING THAT AFTER ALL OF
THAT, THAT ALL OF WHAT YOU HAVE
WAS ABSORBED RATHER THAN BEING POOPED OUT AS THE EXPERIENCE OF LIFE EXPERIENCED BY LUST

51

Dylan.

— o — o — o —

you would think that the word
"Delight" would mean that
there had been light taken away,
rather than the complete opposite;

. . .

lighting up the whole room,
like everyone present had just
scored a Yahtzee 5-of-a-kind
dice roll, with 1-of-a-kind love
Ambulating up
  all Nonchalant and "shucks"
   about owning any of the
responsibility for
   all of that
magnificiently beautiful light.

52824

Family lines
—○——○——○——

my great-grandma DellaLuella
and my great-grandpa James Leroy
have shown up during
the same in-between time that
I have been writing
two books of belonging,
through
the Year-of-the-Dragon;
letting me know that
they approve
of the breathing
that comes from bringing
a Poet to our own
                    familyline.

54

DonKEy JEsus

At Christmas Time
when everyone is excited about Christmas pageants at church,
and all of the traditional favorite tunes of Baby Jesus being born in a
humble manger, you never hear about
the other Jesus who
was born in the very same barn,
on the very same day.

Donkey Jesus.

And, just like Baby Jesus of the manger,
Donkey Jesus still lives today.
It's true.
Donkey Jesus is real.

Coming to the realization that
this is a fact, when nobody until now
has understood, at all, that
Donkey Jesus and Baby Jesus are, in fact,
related by blood
doesn't make it any less true by
believing in the cute one and
just not believing in the other one.
It's still just as true as
the sky is the same blue as
the eyes of beautiful Baby Jesus, wait...
who, upon closer observation,
doesn't have baby blue eyes after all,
not that either Jesus has time for any race-coding,
at all,
so don't get thrown off
by Donkey Jesus
being the blue-eyed one (haha).

Stay with this
with the same level of earnestness,
that Eternity shows you the Truth
of What You Can't See standing in front of you,
even though Truth, being what sets you Free,
is
1 one of the Top 5
Most Essential Things for you to know.
Check the Countdowns
and learn
about

Donkey Jesus.

It only takes a small amount of
time and thinking about it,
no-more-than-a-minute-or-two, really;
the 1 and 2 math (aha!) - Lighbulb Will Get Lit,
as clear as daylight itself does its bit
whether or not
the grey days try to cover up
Halo'd brilliance,
not leaving you
Having to Make Anything Up
about how Truth is Best Understood
when, guess-who presents,
with those clear sky-blue eyes:

Donkey Jesus.

Here's the gig, and I'll get right down to it,
because Donkey Jesus don't like to
wait
for any moments
of toying with nuance.

Halo'd Baby Jesus
of-the-humble-manger

Standing Up,
Looking Right at You
for more than a minute without speaking
with that look that
Knows you Know
Exactly what he's thinking
just as he Knows
you Know Exactly what he's thinking
about what You're Thinking too.

(the Halo'd one, doing that, not the Donkey one)
brothers - but not the same - so we can name them

Halo'd J and Donkey J

to keep their identities distinct;

even on the days
when they wear exactly the same clothing and
Donkey J tries to pass himself off
as the true Halo'd J

you can tell pretty quickly,
without having to factor-in long-distances
because Halo'd J usually stands quietly,
making honestly requested
clarifications
more clear
(with his beautiful-non-blues) while
Donkey J is the guy who grabs
Your Eyes and Attention
through talking with his donkey-arms waving all of the time;
working hypocrisy's ADD-room like a champion
racehorse-conman made happier by
seeing his mark
after seeing you getting confused
about Elementary School
lessons of 1 plus 2;

not learning God's most basic math.
Here, Donkey J
grinning dollar-sign-wide
with silky-milked-hair and
pretty blue eyes
saying
I'm Ready to be your 1-on-1 tutor,

see,
Donkey Jesus is the guy
who knows - without saying
that he's
kinda like that
Pin-the-Tail-on-the-Donkey
game
that everyone plays when they're kids,
except that, with grown-ups, he's their own,
never-kept-private
Donkey Jesus.
Standing in line carrying
detached slips of
unrelated-tale-shaped-paper,
and blindfolds;
secured to
each others' hands and heads
(leave the hearts out of this) then
spin - spin - spin-around-in-the-spin - and
thumb-tack that list of
pre-labeled paper-punch-out preacher-tails
onto wherever the peach-fuzzed-butt is
for Donkey Jesus.

He'll remain extraordinarily still,
taped to the party-wall,
waiting, with his museum-ready-masterpiece
warm, closed-mouth gentle smile while the long line of
stumbleacrossandovereachothertogettherefirst grown-ups
lurch at Donkey Jesus with what they want Him to say is His.

Nailed-it
then, the Braying-Braying-Braying
that never ends.
Please, Halo'd Jesus, if only you could help
the Donkey Jesus people to add
their sincerely held religious beliefs to
God's 1 and 2 math.

Still,
be warned even further,
there's another (completely unrelated but still completely real) Jesus
who is
way-worse.
JackAss Jesus
who doesn't even pretend with parlor games of pinning anything
on paper donkeys or prop-bibles;
not giving the first - middle - or last shit about
last suppers and breaking bread when there's only enough time to
grab handfuls of power and cash while shouting
"Fuck your Feelings 'cause JESUS!"
Glugging
Gethsemane's wine-blood
and throwing the broken-bread-basket
on the floor
on the way to praying-photo-ops at moneyed-churches.

It might all seem a little bit confusing, at first, figuring out
which is which, but the more that you

listen
to what
is being
spoken
And shown

You will see how much any of that has to do with
God's 1 and 2 Math,

and see clearly
right through all of that other bullshit,
giving true focus
to-and-from
the beautiful, true love
of the Original
Halo'd
Baby Jesus.

Merry Christmas
(the non-stolen-one)
to Everyone.

Peace on Earth
and plenty of homemade
Christmas cookies.

♡ ♡ ♡ ♡ ♡ ♡ ♡ ♡ ♡ ♡ ♡ ♡ ♡

Fear Not!

"My goodness! My gosh!"
reflexively grasping at the rich
pearl-necklaces of
strongly-held-religious-beliefs'
scripted jerking-off in
a scriptured-hurry to hurl
digging accusations & rocks,
after stopping for prop-tissues,
then doing some grooming by
"Holydirtypanties" and "Bigboobyselfies"
turning invented truths into
shatterproof lest-me-nots of
the selected
group consenses,
creating
commodified happy endings
built from the bedrock and
cornerstone of shuddering waves

of moral elasticity
  arriving with the spiritual
    subtlety of head-on crashes;
smashing museum-glass-protected
  verses in a spray of
      "the holiest us"
        versus
      "anyone outside"
of their religion's bullshit-soluble
principles of self-preservation
after all, truth be told,
Omniscience
Omnipresence and
Omnipotence all need Big Fighters
  to doo doo all over
    what-God-say-to-don't-do
big O-words be damned,
'cause the shlong-swinging
        He would

not do that even if He wanted to
say "Want a hand to go with that
job, it looks really hard
    and I'm happy to help
        with the heavy-lifting."
leaving self-righteousness
    showing-off its
                    stolen-will
        in holy midriffs.

This Is
    the Unshakable Truth
(paid with the blood of the squashed)
from the beginning
of teething,
all-the-way-to
the follow through of commodifying
masses for tithing, because,
the non-prophet's non-profits
have a deity-thingy.

I'm thinking,
with my opened-heart
beating
on-and-on-and-on
beyond
what's comfortable for my ventricles
   to know
   about what people think
   they know,
about how my heathen-blood
could possibly know
that
the best way
to feed
the beautiful slow-build
   of all of that
   open-hearted,
     unencumbered goodness
with, for, and from what goes through
   all people,
   right out-loud,

without fear of how
fearlessness can seem dangerous
to the god-fearing,
is
to-not-be-afraid of experiencing
any of that delicious,
sacrilegious spunk,
just like Jesus did,
before the part
when
he wept;

and then raised the dead.

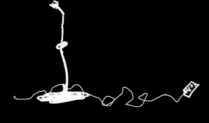

feeling stuff

my terrified soul
does its absolute best
   to tell me
   to not feel because
that's the one thing,
that don't-wanna-feel-specifically-
   that thing, that shakes
      rattlesnake maracas
         at my ankles and feet.
I'm not feelin' any of that without
HOWLING that should only happen
   when I'm looking at the moon;
swelling my face up all puffyred
   or purpleblue the color of
   unable to breathe.
So, Fuck NO to feeling
   anything that would make me
   feel any of that.
I understand my body's traffic signals.

What's that you say?
You can't be serious!
Bonafide-doctorified hospitals
i n t e n t i o n a l l y
administering medicine
to people who have allergic reactions
to that specific med,
knowing that
it could possibly kill them or at=least
   turn their faces into colorbunches
like mine does when facing stuff?
I know what it's like to not be
   able to breathe.
Hospitals are supposed to be helpful
like bomb shelters for sick people,
not places for prescribing dropping
   bombs directly onto their heads.
Doing that
to someone who is already sick:
medical-smack-down
   busted-up bomb-shrapnel
                blood-poison.
How could anyone ever trust that

dropping a medical-allergy bomb
isn't gonna be making things
a wholelotworsethan
it had already been
at home with my brain
letting what needs to fester
fester on... the mighty
hopeless despair hoping
if I let things get
festery enough
they may all eventually die from
brain fever; being ready
with hopefullness showing up at last
to ask pretty please that
while stuff that I don't like 2 look at
finally goes to die... someplace...
please let that happen
without it pulling along with it
any living parts I'm still attached to.

I have learned that we can
(after a pre-auth ego-smash of "I got this")
Learn how to get along with

feeling what we can't-find-a-way to risk
feeling; intentionally introducing
Not That
in an environment of quiet
not-too-well-lit soft
comfortable spot to sit with one
professional mental health person
you can vibe with, and start with
very small doses of
walking
across quicksand

for a little bit.

=
dedicated to everyone within
the mental health community;
helping each other everywhere,
to carefully walk across their
not-thats.

ferocious intention
fed by the feral,
kept-disconnected fury,
looking for anyplace
to plug itself in; feisty
  but trying
to not be
disrespectful
of anyone or anything,
just choosing
wisely
what is worth
respecting.

Everyone's mother has said
"In situations like these,
use your words."

And here we are,
using them;

- - - - - - - -

met
with our eyes
jabbering wildly

while our mouths and fists
form a line and
wait
for their signal
to go ahead.

First and Second Grade Math

If you only had to
    learn-know-remember-do
ANYTHING
that the Holy Bible tells you it cares
    the very most about,
Here's the math:

The Two Greatest Commandments are

1. Love God
2. Love your neighbor

Look it up if you're finding that difficult
    to believe.

Welcome to Bible School Math class.

Flaming Catapult

they used to tar and feather
the unwanted people;
doing true evil to who they'd all agreed
were the truly-true evil,
claiming to know exactly what was
threatening the goodness
  of community,
thinking that god was saying
what it takes
  to show love and devotion
  for all that god has done
  is a good public
humiliation;
not just the barbaric "back then",
  the attempted
  equivalents of →THAT←
still happen today from

non-profit pulpits,
politicians, and
pretty news people, 'cause
Jesus is our favorite fascist.

Tell me none of that is true.

hot-tar-melting-skin

covered with Public Relations'
fluffy feathers,
in a way that could be
fuzzy-jeered at
from safe distances
by the entire community kept
scared grateful,
and sacred;

then, after everyone has

----2----

left,
victorious with
pitchforked
hoorahs,
comes
the careful loosening
of cooled, thickened tar
pulling off layers of
E p i d e r m i s
(a long word for truth that's hated)
being left underfoot in piles,
bloodied and dead with
the sickening experience of
rendering as useless
what was
a human being,
connected with their body's
front-line protector;

Integumentary...
just tryin' to keep it together.

Stripped of this,
the lumped-and-left human's
=immutable spirit=
     not leaving yet, gets lit;
the baptism of fire.
climbing into anti-gravity's catapult,
like a flaming rock in
David's slingshot, built to topple
          infallible giants
pulled-back, taut, to baptize right;
          every bit of human
     wherewithal
completely intact,
understanding that humanity
no longer belonged here.
Saying with a ferocity
     that will never be understood
     by people who stand around
wide-eyed saying nothing, while
watching another balled-up orb of
human-flayed-human...

..glistening with
blood and delicious moonlight,
ready in the x-marks-the-spot, to smile;
saying to the
        stink of soul-captor-wannabees
and sheepish-go-along-with-anythings
"Go ahead and hit launch, motherfuckers."

Beautiful Freedom.

never really knowing how to fly,
    before this;

    the floating glow of
embers

        at another book burning...

the fuck I am
—o—o—o——

There is nothing
worth honoring
more
than the truth of what you
honestly know
you have found to be true,
and are finding
to be the most honorable.
Let the truth
of what others who
try to decide what is true
for everyone
be for themselves,
not for you;
leaving the version of making
something worth honoring be
for them to do, without you,
using their own goddamn rules.

Ghost writer

You are not invisible to me.
I see you
because, like you, I used to think in
invisibilizing terms
through the defining means of
  so many others ahead of me,
but I just couldn't
(or didn't know how to)
keep on going with
not being seen.
I love you
and
I believe in you
writing things in your head
  for other people to claim as
  their own brave truths
  about being gay with your
practiced words, while you remain,
for someone else's reason,
invisible.
I see you and I hope that
one someday while

- - - - - - -

you are still alive
you are able to see
yourself
  out loud about owning
  your own words
with a broad smile that gets it
all neon-lit for every
still invisibilized self
to see.

        - poem written for
         my 15-year old self to read,
         in the forever pages
         of my second book
         of writing out loud;
            here,
             for real,
               stronger now.

the gift of friendship

you know when you have
a friend who is 1 of your 5
you can count on one hand,
when enough of anything
doesn't exist for either of
you, and you 2 stick together
for everything that
matters deeply, through times
when it felt like nothing ever
mattered, for lengths of time
further than the anticipation
of how long either of you thought
you would exist

on the day that he says to you
"I'm spitting on it" and you know
you're going to be spitting on it
too

Grandpa Bud had a Boyfriend

Yeah, I said it out loud
and I'll say it again, even though
Nobody else ever wanted to say it.
Grandpa Bud had a Capital-B
    Boyfriend.
Even when
our steeped-in
family religion, over-ruling
    generations of man love
        with silence
could have helped save my own life,
quietly left riddled with an
ingrained suicidal shame of being gay
while the truth of Grandpa Bud's
    concrete love of a man
remained righteously unspoken.
This loudmouthed kid, though,
coming out through outright
confession to religious leader-men

--- 1 ---

rather than living within
the unbearable weight of nature
  remaining hidden in
that unsurvivable camouflage.
  call me a coward.
no one could ever understand
  the purpose of anyone,
especially an unworthy "other-than",
who otherwise
    was so special
        to God and everyone;
such wasted potential
living to ever say anything out loud,
unnecessarily bringing about
  a whole church court
hammering-out another damned
      excommunication.
but that's another poem
this poem is about Grandpa Bud
having a boyfriend
    that everyone knew about

but that no one felt they could
talk about
throughout all of those decades
of unspeakable love
unable to come out
just left on its own walkabout, gone
starved to death for
love's eternal words
and any of life's
eye-contact.
hoping to at least be thought of
as counting
while everyone else counted
on Grandpa not ever saying
"John Midgeley, I love you."
(if that's how you say his name)
out loud.
He existed without love poems
ever being written for him
in ink
until now.

just an "although"
   of Grandpa's
being tolerated
     at a quiet distance
by Grandpa's Grandma's grown kids.
"although"
 again and again
     tolerated much less from
the family who carried the shame
   of his name
left dying
after withering
with limp wrists
 and without any of them
wanting to have anything to do
   with either of those
      two men so in love
So my Grandpa Bud
   took care of everything
John's burial plot
John's headstone
  attending his funeral alone

he stood with his boyfriend
  John Midgeley
whose family of counterfeit blood
  stood stock still
  within religion's safe refusals
unable to acknowledge their
hate-filled misunderstandings of
  either
    god...
      or love...
        leaving them both alone
instead, only seeing what needed
  to remain buried
    and unmentionable.
I see you, John,
  with my Grandpa Bud.
And now there's a love poem for you
  from one of your own, spoken
  from a stage with a microphone.
I see you two finding a way
    of keeping together
  here - now - forever
after you were both safely gone
87

grateful
for another day of getting
out of bed,
earlier than too early
(sleep knowing where my pen was),
when all of those important words
came knocking on my sleeping
brain's door again,
proselytizing
with shiny name badges and
eager promises of truths
that couldn't wait, then
two new poems, here now, born
breathing, reinforcing the fact that
the life of being
a sleep-deprived writer
is just about
remembering to listen.

Happy
watching my beautiful wife
Smiling and gliding through our home
between things that she's doing
for tonight and tomorrow,
looking like a relaxed firefly
who finds ease with her blinking and
never-not-moving, yet
comfortable
settling down with what's kept her busy;
singing made-up songs
to herself and to our dogs
the whole time that she's doing
everything she needs to do and
all that I do is
watch her...
and smile...
    the smile that didn't know
       this could happen; so grateful
for this simple, beautiful life
here together, today,
seeing my beautiful wife singing...

89

I don't know
how many times
writing has saved my life;
enough times to know
to keep on doing it
even though
sometimes it feels as though
there's more sadness and stuff
than there are places for it to go.
I don't know
why
mental health is so difficult
for people to talk about
making it even more
difficult to even
begin talking
about
the stuff that is in fact truly difficult
to talk about, but
maybe
this ice-breaker of me
raising my hand and

saying out loud
"Hey.
my head gets fucked-up sometimes
and needs
more help
than it would like to admit"
will help,
at least a little bit,
anyone else who also has a tough time
raising their hand and
saying any of that
can't-say-that-stuff-out-loud
stuff;
like I am right here
right now.
Breathing it...
with you...
us two for a minute of
it's ok if I don't know how.

Imagine finding
your favorite thing to do, and then,
at the same time,
being surrounded by people
who love doing
that same thing that you do,
inspiring you
as they do their favorite thing
to do too.
Thank you,
my poet friends at
Austin Poetry Slam.   62624
You are everything
great
coming together,
all happening at exactly the right time;
already
in my mind,
you are what I find
irreplaceable.
                                    dedicated to:
All of the Beautiful Poets at APS

= Thirty Years =
= of Motherfuckin' TENS! =
Congratulations Austin Poetry Slam!

Jason
Edwards

Sean
Patterson

Forney
♡

Jasmine

Micailah
OCaii ♡

K.C. BREEDLOVE

inna minute

waking up too early again
to the quiet demands of words
lining up and taking turns
licking my nose while I sleep.
At least they're not rude
with each other
making room
for latecomers who appear
tugging a ballooned word's
gentle urgency.
after 30 more minutes of
their no longer cute
incessance, listening,
and saying
ok already.

In the beginning was the Word
and the Word was made flesh,
made Beautiful;
Jesus, the only begotten,
thought of as Holy,
wholly to be
spiritually-gang-raped by
nationalism and theocracy rubbing their
junk together, in a reverse exorcism of
immaculate conception, forming
their own halo'd
manifest Destiny and exclusive rights
to heaven; made for white people with
pitchforks, tiki torches and unholy
rage in the name of Jesus; salvation,
locked and loaded. Spirit-leader buddy-team
Holy-Pocket-Pickers, and Soul-Munch,
pouring out public prayers (stick your hands up)
to push our Halo'd J. to stage front
because saving hopeless souls with prayers
takes piles of televangelism cash
(God's love language being money)
leaving Halo'd J. doing a tap-dance
that leaves him nearly dead from
money-grubbed exhaustion,

––– 1 –––

95

but counted on
   to Rise Again in time for
the next mega-church mortgage payment,
   Holy-Ghost-Healing-CEO-bonus, and
   uh-oh, the upcoming elections too,
'cause nationalist take-overs ain't cheap,
      at least not trash-heap-cheap
just striving to be better than anyone
who doesn't believe the right things
(by and for the delightfully pasty)
Political-Operatives-for-Jesus who claim
   They own Him.
Some poor devils gotta pay
   for the soul-smash-and-grab it takes
to be successful in this Holiness-Business!
It gets competitive out there and there's
   only so-much-Jesus
         to go around.
Who knew Christianity's consciousness
   could get so cramped with
holier-than-thous dousing themselves
   in crown-of-thorns perfume.

96 How about this... ----?----

Here's some bear-spray for your face,
        motherfuckers.

We're taking Jesus to our
        Safe House
            of love and worship,

giving him some healing time,
        for who he really is,
        and what he really says,
            to be re-discovered.

Jesus, the original Halo'd J,
probably still wanting to take your calls,
    of course; 'cause Jesus saves,
after all,
        saying, through his busted-up
                    bleeding face, and
            so many holy, broken ribs,
"You're forgiven.

for,
You know not what you do."

Inspirational thought

does pulling my pants down
and wrapping my bare legs around
roof guardrails of cool metal 40-stories up,
then
hanging my bare.ass off of that
                building's backside
    and letting a night-dump-drop
                        airborne, counting
One-one-thousand,
Two-one-thousand
Three-one-thousand then
hearing that happy "PLAP!" at a satisfying
    volume
make me a punk,
or is that just showing up
with no plan and spontaneously following
uncorroborated maps through
        neuropathic nature walks,
            discovering unexplainable
                somethings
                that would be fun to do
without adding
    any 24-hour flourescent-lit pitstop
vending machines selling nothing but
others' pre-packaged question marks.

It is written...

forgive
and forget is logical to keep
in that order for a reason,
not to mean that
you can't
reverse what is
meant by
the proper order of things,
and forget about it first,
before anything else happens again
and adds to your decomposing smile,
it just takes(squashes)takes(squashes)
takes a whole lot longer(squashes)
to do it that way, in reverse order;
better off for at least trying,
knowing the weightlessness of knowing
there's no such thing as time, and
anyway, it's for you, not the person
you're not forgiving, wait,
          what were you saying?

          ...so let it be done.

"It isn't what it isn't"
isn't ever the follow-up that is
said after someone says
    "it is what it is,"
at least I think that it isn't.
I hear it is what it is
all of the time; the "could we go
    —even— one-day—
without one person saying
it is what it is for once" version
of hearing it all the time.
Everyone does it, and everyone
    needs to stop it. Please,
I beg all of you to kill
the fuck-outta-that-fuckin' cliche.
We're at where we're at and that's
    where we'll start with it. Ok...but
there's good stuff that's happening that
    people don't ever talk about, when also
        it isn't what it isn't.

Juneteenth 2024

Start with the fact that Juneteenth is
a whole lot more than a day. In fact,
you couldn't even write a poem
about Juneteenth,
even if you really really tried,
in a day, and you shouldn't even
try
to write one at all
if you're white.
So don't pretend to understand
a goddamn thing about it, when the whole
spectrum
of where you're coming from,
consists of peckerwood-whitey, just like me,
'cause white folks need to know when to
shut the fuck up and listen for awhile;
like, for a long, long while,
with the ears of children
who are learning language for the first time
before knowing any words at all, except,
unlike cute little babies, while we are
learning
any of our first words to speak,

there ain't anything cute
about all of the goo-goo-ga-ga
coming outta white people
talking about it or not wanting to talk about
any of it
even for a minute, so justshutthefuckup to
ALL
know-It-All-When-You-Don't-Know-shit
white people
for awhile, shutting our jabbery mouths for
long enough

to learn
about relevance
in a room full of Beautiful Black Poets.

Juneteenth

now, go do a spirit search
for John Brown

Kuba

that time when everything
that was important
was done exactly the right way
by someone you love, and then,
you thanked them the
wrong-stupid-wrong way, tanking it
by messing up with what always
    makes you think

        here I go
            with my most familiar
            dance step
                one step forward
        two steps back
again on this worn-down ground,
    then,
        being - given - the - grace of
=being Kuba'd=
        and not having to go back
        to fix anything; just
                getting to breathe
from right where I'm at and continue
        moving forward

kissing

—⸻o⸻⸻o⸻⸻o⸻⸻o

Becky,
both of us still in 2nd grade,
being my
first regretful cave-in to peer pressure
convincing me, before even one kiss,
to continue playing the field;
the only 7-year-old male who
took that to mean being serious
about playing and intentionally
losing at kissing tag
during every playground time
with any and every girl
who would join me.
Bold with lip-locking at 7, and
already old enough to know
to be scared about wishing
boys would know how to ask boys
if they'd like to kiss each other too,
without worrying about getting
smashed in the face.

— — — — — — —

yeah...
I guess I was at the head of the class
about all of that; not stopping me from
always wanting to be kissing...
Somebody.
Learning how
          to really-really-kiss
during church dances
while everyone else danced
far away from where
my girlfriend for the next 2 hours and I
were hidden;
not stopping; even when
      being discovered by the other
      teenage school kids, and
      no matter what #1 disco song
      (knock on wood) started playing;
finding out that making hickies
makes everything else
disappear; the way that looking at
hidden stashes of
gay porn
    did the same thing.

I still remember her name too.
No guy names mattered, yet.

Three-way stop-light make-out;
two girls and me tellingtonguetwisters
all three of us all at once in our
connected-mouth-tickle-caverns
until the stopped car that was stuck
behind us when the
            outside light went green
honked and we blasted
      still wishing that we had been
4 with at least 1 person
      besides me beside me who had
scratchy-scruffy-stubble-whiskeries
      to smashanrubbbb allovermyface
drowning myself in male pheremones;
      the perfect way to go...
Hoping that that one-guy-out-there,
like me,
wanted to do a whole lot more
than harpooning.

left with leaving

It has taken too long

to make those

who I am irrelevant to

irrelevant;

left

with leaving with

what is left.

(life's) Open Mic (leaps)
up on the stage,
Spittin'

"not-new shit."
(brief pause, for a breath...)

not-new
shit!!!

"spilling while
unable to answer
heaven's request
psychotetic
promise from
holiest...
from scriptures,
meant for only...
tongue, who'd never go"

drops self to the floor for a moment,
room gasping, stands back up
brushes off leaves.

Living out loud isn't just something
    we do once a year when we
put on a rainbow shirt and
    look hate straight in the eye.
It's by living out loud while
    having the audacity
        to believe in your worth
            as a person, when
no one wants to look at you.
To live through denying
    any-and-everyone the power
= to decide for you =
            = what love means, =
through
throwing sticky gobs of group shame
guiding whether or not you should
allow yourself to feel any
    and all of that beautiful
        love,
        for yourself or for anyone.

To know that you don't have to ask
   to live your life
   fully.
That you can have a full life
   without having to have
   all of the answers,
while also knowing that
you don't have to answer to anyone,

That's what we mean when we say
   =WE are=

      =Celebrating=

         with

      =PRIDE=

living with the undead

denial is still here.
its comically large no-easy-out button
blinking bright red
with overdue life
balances, betting you'd gamble with
not taking a gamble and just
pull the covers up over your head
paying with someone elses interest
in life-saving matters and
another day of instead, just
waiting to die while denial pulsates
mocking you rather than you risking
casting its untrustworthy-unweighted
die, an addict, not daring to face or
fight scary-even-numbers head-on;
stuck
under undercover-blankets in dirty underwear,
bartering for bargains:
smells of breathy-filth for
softening chemicals;
paying-off a little more debt, this time,

with the bloodletting of tomorrow's
   borrowed neverminds that don't
   matter.
so stubbornly reliable,
the blinking-eye-billing-cycle of
denial pushes ahead, anyway
bearing its heirlooms while telling you
to pawn the rest of yours.
waiting another minute,
   to be nice about it, and then
   rolling right up again with its
     nine crusted-over lives to say
       hi...threatening to stay without
       squinting, at the very least
         longer than heaven's best
           guest would be welcome;

just here.
blinking and misbehaving as though
an invitation had been extended
because of looking at it...for a second,
then,

laughing out loud as you push your fists
into your head
trying to deny denial itself.
Such absurd thoughts...
...of dropping heavy-deep
     covers to the old, grimy floor
        and following
           that trail of blood
              down its twenty
                 creaky, wooden steps
                    into the cold concrete
                        basement
can only be met face-to-face when
shoulder-to-shoulder with a friend who
knows that neither of you will say BOO
   to the other as you look at the broken,
   unlatched and blood-smeared corner-
   window, its thick, comfortable,
   cobwebs, already tresspassed,

wondering together,
with the safety of each other,
what happened.

writing love letters'
heart-drum-beats
in-my-sleep
to Jesus, dancing with his halo
writing glowing love-alphabet
letters all around his head
in light trails to me
saying aint-gonna-ever-drop
this sick as shit
loverhythmgroove
with you,
my dude

messenger turtle

I am not having a painful day today
although there is nothing of pain
that I have ever felt about anything
that would approach with a whacking-
stick the fight or flight instincts
I get when old sadness approaches,
  seeing me
with its   bullseye
        of unwelcome insights.
That's not happening today.
I'm onto it now,
  with all of those wide, weepy-eyed
tricks trying to get me
to consider just one more sample
of its loving
teaspoon-sized bites
without worrying about the whole
    wailing thing again.
I can't.
It still breaks me in half and that
  knowledge is power.
  I KNOW THAT
just like before

even one measured dose
will pull itself through my bloodstream
like a corkscrew virus taking over
conduits built for sustaining life and
turning them into its own
amusement park ride; intentionally
jumping the rails, bent on crashing
my own quietly grieving blood cells
with its dead-ends of getting stuffed
into a locked suitcase that
I can't get out of any other way than
letting go of myself
again
just to find the same old me
again; those rubber-banded luggage
toe tags, indicating something belonging
ripped off.
Even with all of the preparation it takes
for avoidance of everybody
and everything,
there is still nothing
        more terrifying
            than feeling
nothing.

walking through
   such desolation
      keeping anything of myself intact
while looking for signs of any worthwhile
part of my life-like-looking for
bacteria's miracles
through the dusty surface of Mars,
while still
smiling all of the time because
no one must know
   that
my planet-rover
         got stuck on a rock... again,
then, some random
reassurance from the Multicolored Universe
says with its glittered space-dust
"You don't have to understand anything
   other than to keep moving."
I was never good at math.
but I know that
somewhere, in some galaxy-calculator,
this shit will add up
         to something
               that matters
   if I can just keep my heart...

...and my integrity together
while looking for signs on that rickety
bridge
I'm
moving
across
high
abo
v
e

the shit that I don't want to ever feel
and the vertigo that I get
from feeling nothing.

inevitable; that shit-ton smackdown
when the bridge unravels, and drops
leaving all of my breath
in the
air up there
all lonely without me breathing it...

...from where I am, on the ground-level
  floor, all ground-down, every bone
  broken and melting into
the resettling dust-storm of bright
realization that fight-and-flight have
   teamed up and
vanished with every drop of daylight,
allowing that fucked-up
          never-gonna-give-up
sadness
to weave
its slow nourishment into the pores of
my broken body.
Jarring
how comforting that reassurance can be
during your own bloodletting of feeling
one-word-at-a-time;
freely given,
written or spoken,
the comforter and the comforted both
knowing exactly what
          lettersmash sounds like
when all of your consonants are broken.

got the message, mr. turtle.
thank you.
just don't leave me here
because I need to be able
to put at least some of these
broken consonants onto
...the writing paper that could...
help me
or anyone
to hitch a ride forward.

my voice has a place
for this time in the human race's
life. finding itself after
the body of the woman who
taught me how to read
and write before I was five
(my two favorite things to do)
had died. Oh, how I hope
that somehow
she knows, the same way that
Moms know everything,
that her little kid
who struggled to figure out
which letter the word "refrigerator"
started with,
now has his first book being kept
on the shelves
of the local library.

3624

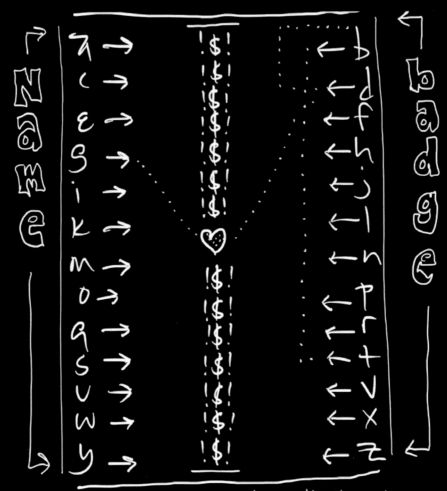

CREATE a dot-to-dot path, with the only way to get across to the other half of the alphabet being through the heart, all other paths being blocked by money and power; spell your name, your friends' names, your hopes and values, the U.S. Constitution. Then, removing money and power's interference, see how much easier and less messy it gets, and, see how half of the alphabet no longer looks like the enemies of the other half every time you just want to be able to spell stuff.

name badge

a → →
c → →
e → →
g → →
i → →
k → →
m → →
o → →
q → →
s → →
u → →
w → →
y → →

!$!
!$!
!$!
!$!
!$!
!$!
!$!

♡

!$!
!$!
!$!
!$!
!$!
!$!
!$!

← b
← d
← f
← h
← j
← l
← n
← p
← r
← t
← v
← x
← z

practice
area
♡

not erasing people

guess what
I'm not gonna sit
and let you erase
people
who I love, without
sitting down
and writing a poem
about that, and
about them, and
about you
wandering off thinking
that your work here
was done.

the first time that I felt
nothing
was while listening
to my big brother asking
my broken father
to not leave us
again.

Now

every day feels like already
which is proof
(or at least evidence) to me
that I haven't jumped out of
time's deep track.
the thing
for me to remember as I am
putting today's math
together
is that Now
is the only word on the matter
on time's infinity-wide-spectrum
that matters;
with its cool,
sparkling clean
artesian spring fountains
... continuous
everything...

Old People

How many multipliers
do you think you were born with
Little crackerjack,
when you didn't even know
that those
little caramel popcorn boxes
used to have real prizes in 'em.
You never knew what
you were gonna get,
kinda like your multiplier,
in a way.
Well, guess what, and
wake back up for this important
stuff;
I've got a pretty good idea
what mine is, by now,
my multiplier, that is, and it was a lot;
like way way wayyyyy better
(that's how people talk now, right? I'm
   just tryin' to keep you engaged
in conversation; using familiar language

...an old trick. Hah!)
no?
ok, I'll give up on the making jokes part.
Teachable at bizillion-and-three
Look at me! oh, I did it again?
Ok, I'll calm back down (but not out)
(hah! I snuck that one in!)
moving on...

refer to page
one for
clarification
if you must

... way way better
(multipliers add their own "wise"... hah!)
ok ok, trying harder this   gotcha.
time. way better   again!
than any used-to-be-greats of
wondering what prize you'd find
by digging through the sweet stuff
in a big hurry to.
get to the emptied box
 looking at pre-packaged trinkets
you couldn't keep once you
 dropped, alongside the emptied box
  anyway.

I'm still living
in the holy now just like you.
The way that we see everyday.
Although, with old people,
in case you didn't know, our stories
have developed, with all of us
"going all the way to eleven" and
   allowing ourselve's the love and the
   attentive caring to our life stories
      is how we show, to ourselves,
            respect for elders.

having more
      ring-of-treetrunk-layers
than we could have ever known about
   ahead of time
beyond unquantifiable multipliers
   of beginning
      of wishing
         of searching
            of breaking and finding
            and breaking again
            and finding again
            and

loving everything within the beauty
the corniness and the sadness of
these time-doesn't-exist-days
that don't want to be left but that
get left anyway... the beauty... and the
love... never goes away... when you're
really wanting to hang onto it
just a little bit longer, even now,
long enough to have one,
two, or two thousand moments as
spectacular as everything that
never had words before,
before you're ready to
really let go   in a way
that you're not sure what will
happen next; but you know

that it's time.
                              ^ go already,
         not ^   ^ to go it?
            really   is it?
so   fuck
grateful   no.
for the holy now
with my Fredricksburg
family of old people...   ♡

130

the person you are
when
no one else is around
is the person
that
you
really are.

play the music
you've been waiting to hear.

you know.
that one song that
you know by heart;

on that upright piano of yours that
you and I both see, unmoved,
sitting in the middle of the
car-blurred-autobahn,
its heart quietly tapping at 4/4,
also waiting for your music

before seatbelt people
make toothpicks.

7224

...playing outside
without falling
into any of the holes
th t h ve l een du
a a >   g

by those who
are on the inside...

pocket change

if you split
your family's generations of
  tradition-pants at the
  but-seems,
don't forget to first empty the day's
        =true treasures=
from your deep-pockets
    of soul-splitting-grief
before those old-worn-out
          inside-out-and-backwards-pants
get self-depantsed and
        =look! no hands!=
chucked through the opened window of
your stolen-back speeding-away
  soul-automobile.
fuck paying someone elses toll roads
  with your own pocket change;
pay time and attention
  to noticing
    how fantastic
      that breeze...

feels like this...
as it flies through
your newly liberated boxers.
nearly anything
more than nothing is
MILLIONS of times better than
the regret of remaining
in the re-gifting traditions of
all of those uptighty-whities
cutting off any chance of
circulation until gone
all the rest of the way dead.
go ahead and
let that flying bird fly;
catching waves of wind currents
with your cupped hand
through the unrolling window,
u^{P}a$_n$d^o^{w}$_n$a$_n$d^u^{P}a$_n$d^o^{w}$_n$
opened.
flying outside.

Identity
(pŏp-qŭĭz)

1. telling anyone that they don't understand their

—i d ɛ n t i t y—

better than you do; you, who likely doesn't even know who the human is who you're claiming to know better than themselves and their

— ɛ n t i r ɛ —

—i d ɛ n t i t y —

is an example of (select one):

a. Donkey Jesus

hint: remember, people got pissed off when Halo'd Jesus told them his true identity too.

2. Going to city council meetings, or already being an elected "official" yourself, and making <u>policy</u> decisions about someone's
— i d e n t i t y —
being so important to <u>you</u> that <u>you</u> need to enforce how a whole group of humans can/can't move through
— their life —
Especially if your reason for being a complete dumbshit asshole is "because Jesus"; claiming that in order to "protect" your (or anybody else's) kids, that nobody even asked them to have, somehow has you in God's own, (not so)
Secret Service
on a holy crusade to dehumanize, vilify and erase rights due to a <u>human's</u> <u>identity</u> (select one answer):

a. Jack Ass Jesus

my potential
for not intentionally ending

surfaced

while I was
not paying attention
to its constant bickering,

by
stepping outside
and looking

for ways of being

of service.

Hey Punk!

Do you see
That dried-out
Boulder
Sitting
Way up on that
Geological
High priest High-Chair
Like it has belonged and been
There forever?
Climb up there.
And kick that smugmotherfucker

O,,

«⅄⅄

«Λ,,

puppies
looking at the moon
while everyone is sleeping.

here, queer, and happy
to bring an answer
to anyone's querying
about how it is so
necessary
for us (not just about you
although you might also
be a part of the equation)
to be showing the whole world
the equality
that we have a right to,
with Pride.

safe and unsound
— o — o — o

there was a guy
who stole

a gay pride rainbow flag
from the front of
a church showing support
for our LGBTQ+ community.

He said that it had violated
his religious freedom...

... stealing beliefs
from another church...

Maybe that's why state governments
want so badly
to force public classrooms
to prominently display replicas
of ancient, burning bush produced
stone tablets; just in case the
opportunity arises for a
true stoning.

shelter

Junior Lily
Brownie & Sydney & Bindi
BEETHOVEN
Bandit Salt & Pepper chance
Lucy Stevie Emily Kenzie
Colt Elsa
Roman Bella Bobby Snoopy & Ozzy
Spud & Peppermint Moose
Patty Austin Dino
Izzy Delilah JT TBdG
Juliet & Tyler Kelsey Molly
Ghost Liberty Rose

please adopt, foster, volunteer,
and/or donate with your
local animal shelter
♡ ♡ ♡ ♡ ♡ ♡ ♡ ♡

smile
just that.
that swear word you won't
even let yourself think, at
the beginning of this poem.
it's ok to do that thing...again;
even right out in the open,
right in front of anyone,
without apologizing and
without even remembering
to feel bad
about not remembering
to still feel bad
for a minute.

stretching the seems

if it seems that someone is
always upbeat,
the positive one,
it may be because
they're worried about
how far they'd topple-down
if they ever let themselves
let go and feed
the big sad.
So...
Sometimes
it splits-through
double-stitched
seams with
hard-elbows.

sweet terrarium sweat

like a window that is
being
licked with summer
love felt
from living

inside of a terrarium;
you can go
wherever you want to go, while
I will be here, soaked
in beautiful Texas,
alive, right where I'm at,
with glitter-dot fireflies
and meditative cicadas.

take time to matter
and allow for the time that it takes
for something or someone
or a whole lotta everything to matter
    to you. It doesn't matter if you never
have enough time for what matters.
This is your motherfucking time;
motherfucking take it. It's yours.
Don't ask first and don't apologize and
put down your goddamn phone unless
it's to call someone who matters.
You are not your job, your trauma,
your fancy-ass car or your
no-motherfucking-car-and-your-bike-
    motherfucking-got-stolen.
You are not what any other motherfucker
    thinks about you.
Fuck them and let them run free.
I'll bet that you matter to someone
    who you don't even know
    you matter to, but even that
    won't matter if you don't
    check-in with yourself
    for long enough to motherfucking
    matter to you too.

Although,
I've gotta motherfucking say this
  motherfucking part out loud,
      because being at either or
    both ends of what quietly matters
the most,
          is to allow steep as fuck
        pre-destination cliffs
      that you'll walk right up to

                                    and

                                  walk

                                    o f

                                      f

into the unbelievable
          of motherfucking knowing
that living longer than you thought you would
means being the only one left
    in the original picture of
mattering to each other
            in the same breath
        of every breath of knowing
that neither of you can die before the other

and the unlucky motherfucker
who is still stuck here
after the other one goes
is the one who is gonna be left
   motherfucking HOWLING
   knowing exactly what music to play
      before even remembering to
      light a motherfucking candle...
leaving soon anyway...
   so leaving a fire lit in the house
   would be bad...
   to forget about just MOTHERFUCKING
      DRIVE...everywhere
      that you were supposed to SEE
      with me, yelling out the
      car window
         GET HERE.
FUCKING GET HERE AND BE HERE
   WITH ME MOTHERFUCKER
You cannot be gone
You have GOT TO BE HERE with me
PLEASE be here, stay here

with me and be here every
motherfucking day
'cause YOU HAVE GOT TO STILL BE HERE
to yell BOXCARS! BOXCARS! BOXCARS!
with me motherfucking fuck
DON'T BE GONE YET.
It wasn't me that was
supposed to be left
motherfucking crying
like this.

Andrew King
Kevin Morgan
Chris McDaniel
Every motherfucking one of you
motherfuckers better
motherfucking be there
when I get there too.
1969-2004-∞
1972-2017-∞
1970-2024-∞

These insistent words
find their way to the surface
with me in a way
that could easily mislead me
(or any others)
into believing that each of them
being here
had anything to do with me.
They were always
all
gonna get here.
I am only the lucky one
who got to
see them climb from their
kept place, and up through
the silencing surface w first

52424

dedicated to
my library friends; especially Cindy.

this is the tired
that won't let you sleep;
that says if you don't
get up without thinking,
right now,
even while your feet are still
talking about yesterday,
    you will
      begin experiencing
      increasing pain
      on top of your
      tiredness
until you relent,
listen,
and get up
to do it
again.

Thank you, Nashville Warbler
Eastern Phoebe
Carolina Wren
Northern Cardinal
Tufted Titmouse
Song Sparrow
Carolina Chickadee
Benwick's Wren
Black-Crested Titmouse
Yellow-Rumped Warbler
House Finch
and Roadrunner who I didn't know
knew how to sing;
each of you, singing, within
10 minutes of you being here,
with my dog AppleJacks & me.
Thank you.

thoughts & prayers...

saying the word "thoughts"
    is not
    the same thing as having
        a thought, just as
saying the word "prayers",
    or "prayers sent",
    or "praying",
    even when built into
a combo-tray of "hope & pray",
doesn't mean that anyone
        ever did any of those things.
like saying "there are no words",
    using actual words,
    to say nothing. Just skip
the phony phoned-in bromides
and do some shit.
            if you mean it.

to have tiptoed
around everyone else
for

d ε v
i h a ε a r ε d e g n o l
s a p o t   o n ε   v
h g u
ε
n
t
o
m
y
s
e
l
f

That part is over.
Allowing
what
couldn't be
looked at;
to be seen.

today is this...

anointed and ordained

by one perfectly placed

raindrop

landing

squarely

on the crown of my head

while walking

our dogs at five

in the

quiet, dark morning

31724

toddymanners

= that was the seed that lifted me =
= from before I knew =
= what seeds were made of, the seed of =
= a dragon =
= made of fluid blue flying purple and =
= color naming itself its =
= fruit flavor twin =
= one leading vowel's constant =
= shape of surprise and wonder =
= orange =
= hunger kept sated by flying =
= not needing wings =
= in any =
= configuration of movement =
= capable =
= by a dragon just finding out =
= that yes =
= dragons =
= do exist =
= at the same =
= time of finding out =
= that I am =
= one =

$$1 + 1 = 22$$

Learning about love
through the
lack of its absence
while being held
for the first time
is the first
of what is learned about love
after
a child's breathing begins
meaning that,
just as the unknown meanings of
all of those
electrical synapses,
connecting when love
begins, in
the unknowable moment that
love stops...
the breathing could still be
attached to it
left stuck to the

loving-has-gone spot
until the breathing, still
       from where it started
             trying to remain

                            also stops;

left uneven
even if most of
that beautiful loving and breathing
had been internally-sourced to begin with

Then again,
if a child is not held at all,
during early development,
a whole salad bowl of
irreversible
antisocial disorders will ferment
the centers of that unwanted child's
underdeveloped
ability for feeling
caring,
leaving the breathing part

            —— 2————   159

to stand all alone;
strong, without any image
of what-could-have-been-caring
the film left unexposed,
without any pictures to compare anything;
still,
breathing just fine;
finding it impossible
to picture what never existed
to begin with.

unsure of which is worse:

to have never known warmth at all,
or to know it once and not know
how to find it again.

Then,
meeting my Beautiful Soledad
and smiling more than I knew how to
    smile; unceasing, the relentlessness of
so much stuporous joyfulness,

whole arenas of
undiscovered mouth-muscles
became towering fountains of
escaping laughter;
deep springs of artesian water
that had been left untapped;
unknown love resources that
had only been kept trapped,
poking pain into making its
vigorous last stand
through glowing smiles so wide times two
they begged
to let their entire-aching-faces
stop for awhile
while
finding their reasonable minds footing;
mouths doing the mouth stuff they're
more comfortable with doing
again
in this twisted new place where

WE
STILL
COULD
NOT
STOP
LAUGHING

smiles so wide they had to be reminded
to pace themselves...
to run more of that happiness marathon
tomorrow, after adequate training,
lighter shoes,
and a secured supply of
sliding-scale insulin, or
You'll-Never-Know-How-To-Handle-It.
Stop Thinking.
that you could ever
Forget memory's most painful shit
for Even One Moment.
of Uncertainty's future shit

Now wait just a minute.

Gonna go ahead and say yes to this
and a great big
NOPE to fear's lockdown
because every tiny bit of me knows
    = This is love =
    = that is as pure =
    = as love ever is. =

Imagine then,
thinking that I was finally
marrying my man
and finding out,
one year after exchanging
    our engagement for wedding vows
        = BESOS! BESOS! BESOS! =
that 1 + 1 = 22
and the man who
I thought I was marrying = BESOS! =
was in fact
My Beautiful Transgender Woman of Color.
My Beautiful Soledad.

— — 6 — — —

Immediately knowing that
God's math works best when
    not looking in the back of the book
    for the answers when
    Love's Most Beautiful Truth is
        standing
        right in front of me

with her hopeful, matter-of-fact-eyes
and with every
wanna-know-it-all-in-my-brain
asking

"what are you gonna do?"
        as if LOVE
had no say in the matter.
LOVE SO WARM AND TRUE
What the Holy Fuck do you Think
I am going to do, but
Get down on one knee and
Tell Her That
had I already known

about ALL of the Beauty
of her Being
the Beautiful Woman
She had Already been, so worried
about Showing me
Everything,
I would Still Be Right Here
kneeling in front of her,
Asking her if she would
Please Marry Me
=BESOS!=
Hoping that she would say yes
and that
We could Be,
My Beautiful Soledad and me,
siempre juntos y siempre cresciendo
flying hand-in-hand through
our Beautiful and Ever Expanding
Multicolored Universe for
ETERNIDAD

———∞———

ps,

don't think that this means
anyone can start asking us
about fucking,
the same way
that it was never ok
to spend any time puzzling
over anyone's fucking
when anyone thought
we were both men.

Trust
that you don't have to hold onto
this, because this, that is here
today was already here
  when we got here, just like
this today, that is
here with you
in it with me
after you've gone
is also the same today
that will be
here with you
in it with me
again tomorrow.
This is the absolute truth
that has
nothing to do with
          no-such-thing-time;
eternity, already is.

= Drew + Todd + Kevin for 4ever =
_____

167

two wherevers

"wherever the hate is,
let it out.
wherever the love is,
let it in."

the unhiding

Sometimes
writing poems
takes the shape of
unhiding
and lighting bonfires;
setting flame
to toppling piles
of grudged-up grease-rags,
smudged by every miserly kept
should-but-didn't
and shouldn't;
their terrible messes,
wiped off and left
in the left-cornered wads
of not growing up
quite right.
here, alive, now while
the opposites of catch-and-release are
catching fire,
  the toppling
towered-up and lit high
not forgetting about the forgotten
few, unused, but still shaken-up

spray-paint cans thrown into the fire,
saying that they couldn't remember
   how to shake words out
            since the time from
                  before hands existed;

hands
left frozen,
now warmed with flames of
feeling how it feels to be connected
      to what's standing
                  and minding
                  the flaming pile
                  with long sticks
                  as it

   b u r n s
its curled-up stink
to the satisfied ground;

watching downcast shadows
that
   dance
and twist
with their escape
   across my resonant face

while
    t h i c k
        b l a c k
            s m o k e
                c l o u d s

unwrithe;
floating soot
moving away
with familiar silence;
comfortable distance rising
    across the wide
            r e l a x e d   s k y,
poetry...
generous with all of its
    smoke-signaled promises to so many
        uncut veins left more curious;
alive with wondering
about that which is yet
to get pitched.

we are 2 who count

there are two points
to writing and sending to anyone
   in the world
the poems in the books that I write
(feelings getting some new wings).
One: honoring the people, the beauty,
   and the adventures that I have had
in a life
that I didn't always want to live in, and
Two: to help anyone else in the world
   who also
      may not want to live
      sometimes to find
the people,
the beauty, and
the adventures in a life that they feel
happy about staying alive
for today,
just like me,
reaching for
at-least-sorta-sometimes
too.

what poems can do
the way that this one did
for me
when I wrote it
today,
is the reason that
I like to write them.
well,
that, and the fact
that I have no choice

about any of it;
            that is,

if I want
to keep breathing
like this...

when you grow up
with the unspoken understanding
that to leave the straight lines
of your childhood
family religion
without dying
would be
unimaginable,
then, anyone
forcing your
leaving
leaves
you
with
finding
what is
beyond
elephant
tribe-sized
imaginagility

:
:

when you're a writer
———o———o———o———

daddering around
with your favorite pen in your hand
without knowing how long ago,
or knowing at all
that your hand had decided
                to
              =start
            carrying your pen
is the best
of
absentminded experiences
that come with being
a writer;
looking up
and seeing
your dog already all smiling at you,
   who then picks up and follows you
     from room to room, still with
your pen in your hand,
   as you look for a place

to sit down together
and write again; every
once in awhile seeing
your pen locating a hidden map
    to the holy-glowing-grail
while sitting right there with your dog,
then,
sharing peanutbutterapplesnacks.

While I'm awake
I am either writing,
or wishing that I was writing
all of those countless shapes that
keep on flooding my brain,
letting go of time
and losing track of everything,
to figure out how
all of those
letters float apart or
together;
most preferably,
within
the close vicinity
of as many dogs as possible.
there.
now you know me.

no helmet
being that pure link
of such elemental difference,
from sitting
alone in a
pissed bathtub
in the afternoon
to swim-dancing all dolphin-style
synchronized with the ocean's
   vibrance, released from the shore,
unemployed,
carefree and naked
while my best friend
patiently waits
   like always.

   your
      chrome
handlebars shining at the beach
playing on that perfect day.

before my drinking turned into
blackout
undertows
this-many
too-many-times,

and I left you;

double-parked in front of a bar
before stumbling inside
     leaving your keys...
          to be found by anyone...
          right-in-your-ignition
          that we both knew as
only ours while I disappeared for
     so   many   hours
          the   back   alleys
crawled through on all fours 'til
my lightbulb went on and
     coming back
to
only finding
  your
a b s e n c e.

the one thing
i had left
in the world
i could do
was to
     lay down

into the comforting arms of empty
night sidewalk
and cry with the street
until i passed out.
          meltingintotheground.

im sorry.

please find me
  again
if you can.

you may not know me sober,
  at first, but I will know you

with the immediacy of everything
we still are.

... my Shadrach ...

sometimes,
the wet-sloppy gaps
left
in the ground
after
pulling out handfuls
of
sludgey-muck

make a

nutrient-rich-place

for nature

to plant

all of her gorgeous

wildflowers.

<u>Yep, we counted</u>

Inside-Out and
   Backwards met

Can't-Get-Right,
   who was hanging out
      with his friend
         Nobody-No-How
along with a few Other-Than-New
   No-Names

      and because of a
         Strange-Somehow,
through gathering,
   although not through
         with gathering,

nearly all of their broken parts
   found their fit.

feeling fetched

being an old man
with his dog
at the park
(or anywhere else for that matter)
is the happiest version
of belonging

there is.

three infinities

... seeing a woman
who was sitting on the ground
with her legs crossed
in the middle of a planet
handmade with multiple
overlapping chalk-drawn
circles on the concrete
boardwalk at Venice Beach
with bits of trash moved
into very strategic places
within and around
her chalk-circle planet
and her,
so deep in thoughtful
consideration
about where to place
each important treasure
that she had
still cupped in her hands

as a circle of people,
including me,
stood around her and watched,
nearly as mesmerized as she was,
when she suddenly
looked straight up at me
from her cross-legged place
within her safe planet-circle,
having a eureka-moment
seeing me
saying "Robin Hood!
You're Robin Hood!
I have to give you something!"
and looking
everywhere on her planet
for urgent gifts
that were meant for me, and
seconds later, she said
"Here! Three Infinities and some hair!"
putting them all into my opened hand
before I knew what was happening
or what anything meant

186   -------

and seeing her bright, wide eyes
smiling and watching me
receiving her thoughtful gifts;
Robin Hood
opening his hand to look with
blind actuality seeing
whats there:
three
flattened sideways styrofoam shipping peanuts
in the shapes
of number eights
and
a small clump of hair;
whoknowswhose.
Not sure what to do with any of
    these believables
except to smile
and say thank you;
her face
still so excited about
having given her important gifts
to Robin Hood
as I walked away, never forgetting her.

now here,
    four decades later
remembering her as I am preparing
to publish this very book,
    that I never knew would exist, on
August 8, 2024; today's future date
made of three infinities
    with a head full of purple hair
walking through afternoon wildflowers
while poetry walks through my head
    planting handmade planets of
    handwritten words
a whole solar system away from where
I met her; maybe she really did see
    the whole thing happening
        today

Untitled

Grandpa Russ and me being
at the end of his birthday party
after everyone else had left;
the two of us, sitting in wooden chairs
we had placed in front of the
propped-open refrigerator door;
every light in the apartment turned off,
the light from the opened refrigerator
glowing across our faces and into the
circle of light around us
while we sat with our feet up
on the lower shelves of the refrigerator,
party hats still on our heads,
music off,
both of us smiling without speaking while
living within our refrigerator reverie...

Dad, sitting quietly in the middle of
the Mormon Tabernacle choir while

the whole choir was standing & singing.

Mom, being the first person to greet me
in heaven, when I arrived there;
somehow knowing that I was on my way
ahead of time enough to have made
a delicious homemade dinner
for my arrival; smiling her happy Mom smile
when she saw me arriving.

Seeing Drew at a party
in a room full of guys. Wearing a
perfectly-fitted clean white t-shirt
and a great big smile.
Everyone in the room celebrating something.
Us, catching each other's eye-contact
from across the room with everyone
in a constant swirl of movement
around each other; both of us
immediately locking-in with every molecule
of our love again; like there
had never been a day in-between,

190
— — — — — — — —

having smiles so huge and true that
anyone witnessing us seeing each other
would immediately know the joy
we were both feeling
when Drew disappeared into the group of
dancing men; waking up
the next morning with his giant smile and
beaming eyes still in my minds place
for new memories.

Cliff diving with Kevin, out of nowhere,
like we had both materialized there
from wherever we'd been up until then,
shoulder-to-shoulder,
both of us already wet from jumping
at least once before that,
smiling smiles and smiling eyes
times both of us, counting 1...2...3...
   JUMP!
      launched
         flying
            plunged

through
the cool, deep water;
   splashdown-currents flying-up
   all

      around us

Imagining and hoping
that when it is also my time to go,
that the people around me who I love
   and who love me will be finding me
the way that I somehow found
my grandpa, my dad and
      Mom, Drew & Kevin
for the yet untitled adventure
   we'll get to have together,
   helping them to know
      I'm still here
      with them

      for all of it.

and then with
a sticker star
the universe said

✦ you are here.

I love you JESUS the only begotten
...one...

you're my
favorite person of color.
Thank you for still being here
with me (and then Jesus said:)
"you're welcome. I love you too,
and since I know that you have
been liking haikus lately, I've got one
for you (better be ready 'cuz it's a good one
jus' like you and me... ready for this?)

the rock rolls away.
Jesus, glowing with laughter,
yelling "April Fools!"

"Are you serious with this, Jesus?"
"Died for your sins 'cause of loving you,
serious. Is that serious enough for you?"

"Fuck yeah!" I said.
Then we hugged,
knuckle-bumped, and walked away;
both of us still laughing...

194

the music from

some of those

kept-missing parts

is now free

to be here,

accompanying

today's

breeze;

though

still not here,

no longer

kept-missing.

...more shapes...

———o———o———o———

...memorizing Doctrine's Covenants section 4 at 18-years old during early Sunday Morning Missionary Prep class with Brad...

...12 years later, after my Mission, excommunication, and finding myself in recovery from alcoholism yelling "Stonewall was a riot! Not a fucking t-shirt!" with Stella Francis Louise, both of us wearing skirts, marching with our fists raised through the streets of New York City...

...eventually finding that there was no incompatability or incongruence between these two defining elements of who I am...

———————

...Erin casually eating a miniature cupcake like it was being tossed back from a shot-glass, on a day when everyone was trapped in sadness, all of us momentarily being whiplashed into laughing again...

...seeing Erin being such a beautifully attentive, loving Mom to her young son, reminding me, every time, of how my own Mom always was with me when I was still her little kid, and how that never did change as I grew up; memories with her still being the greatest treasures of my life...

...the universe saying *you are here with a mama deer and her new baby walking together through the morning...

... our little-little one, Jesús, sitting
on my beautiful Soledad's chair, his
fuzzy ears perked up with listening
to his mama Chole's beautiful voice,
singing a song from another room;
a beam of sunlight shining perfectly
through the window next to him,
lighting up his perked up furry ears...
... my beautiful Applejacks lying in
front of my lava lamp, next to
me while I write, both of us
mesmerized...
... seeing my beautiful Soledad from
a distance, without her seeing me
watching her, wearing her floppy-
brimmed sun hat walking our little
one and our little-little one along
a tree-lined path; their time of
being together so complete together,
so beautiful, the life that we've found

200 - - - - - - - ...

...finding my way out of a gone-sour first-(too) long-term relationship, after going back to it again-and-again-and-again, by putting a post-it note to myself in my wallet, where I'd written "you didn't get yelled at today"...

... Someone asking me "if you treated your friends the same way that you treat yourself, how long would they be your friends?"...

... finding a way to start a new life, with a new post-it note in my wallet that said "you are valued"...

...Painting the words to Bjork's song "all is full of love" along a winding path all across the ceiling where Drew & I lived together on christmas Tree lane...

...Mom, making homemade
christmas cookies and lighting
her Chrismas candles while
listening to the Mormon Tabernacle
choir singing "The Joy of Christmas",
having the sequence of songs
memorized from so many repeated
plays of the record, she'd start
singing the first few notes of the
next song coming up, during the
gaps between each song...

...sound activated mood lights
flashing along with the rhythm
of booming Texas thunderstorms...

...my dogs coming to me for comfort
and the reassurance of safety
during thunderstorms or fireworks;
realizing that I'm their reliable
guy, helping them to know they're
alright during scary times...

... spittin' my "gay shit" and
"Grandpa Bud had a Boyfriend"
poems on a stage in front of a
live mic, live audience, and on a
livestream to wherever-in-the-world,
the absolutely-real, opposite-end of
a light-bridge from anything I
would have ever imagined myself
doing while being the deeply closeted
teenage kid in "ghost writer",
terrified by the churchified-rumor
that my deepest, most shameful secret
of being gay gay gay gay gay
would someday be shouted-out by
angels on rooftops, calling me out
for being a terriblesinnerpervert...

...living long enough to reach my
butterfly year during the year of
the dragon...
                      ...playing my banjo
on a meditative rolling-loop for
my dogs and me...

- - - - - - - -   203

...seeing and being slow cheetahs with my sister Johanna...

...Lefty the greek bartender's rooftop in Firenze at sunrise...

...Easter sunrise service at the Hollywood Bowl; Frankie Goes to Hollywood there, the same year...

...meeting Debbie Harry, Nina Hagen, and Carrie Fisher...

...Madonna wearing my hat in Italy...

...wishing that I had gotten to see the Clash, anywhere...

...Everyday of living on our shared rooftop in Long Beach with David...

...phad thai on Voyager nights with Drew.

...Battlestar Galactica nights with Kevin and our crew...

...Daniel Martinez, Scott Haycock,
and Ron Boyer...
... Tony & Daniel...
... Don & Roscoe...
... Lukebutt...
...John Pepperoni, Kenny H., and Ken A...
... Tracy Gay and Doug Ann...
...Peter Bragino connecting the
dots and breathing from within
every dimension of creativity's
possibilities...
... learning about maintaining
personal integrity and doing
the next right thing while
insisting on being happy, joyous
and free, from Troy Caperton...
... Lisa buying me a set of work
clothes, telling me "go get a job
you're not going back."

ps,
      just like we did at the
aint-gonna-end at the end of
my book before this, I've saved
a few pages for you to write

... more of
         your shapes...

            ☆ here

made eternal...
      the moment...
            they were born...

  ...
                        ...

and the truth shall set you free today

Made in the USA
San Bernardino, CA
25 September 2017